JEWISH BEDTIME STORIES & SONGS FOR FAMILIES

**The PJ Library**® is happy to share with you this sample of the free, high-quality books and music sent to participating families every month. Each book comes with customized flaps that provide a Jewish framework for that selection.

**Join the growing, global PJ Library community --**

## ENROLL TODAY

# www.pjlibrary.org

A PROGRAM OF THE HAROLD GRINSPOON FOUNDATION

*For my son, Ira Reuben, and for Mrs. Zians, who showed me the joy of a Shabbat Box. — LS*

*To my mother. — NB*

KAR-BEN PUBLISHING
A division of Lerner Publishing Group, Inc.
241 First Avenue North
Minneapolis, MN 55401 U.S.A.
800-4KARBEN

Website address: www.karben.com

Shabbat (the Jewish Sabbath) comes every week. It is a time of joy and family celebration. On Friday at sundown, Jewish families welcome Shabbat by lighting candles and saying blessings over wine and challah (braided bread). On Saturday after sundown, Shabbat is concluded with Havdalah prayers.

Library of Congress Cataloging-in-Publication Data

Simpson, Lesley.
      The Shabbat box / Lesley Simpson ; illustrated by Nicole in den Bosch.
           p.    cm.
      Summary: When it is finally Ira's turn to take his nursery school class's Shabbat Box home, he loses it in a snowstorm and must decide what to do next.
      ISBN-13: 978-1-58013-027-1 (pbk. : alk. paper)
      ISBN-10: 1-58013-027-5 (pbk. : alk. paper)
      [1. Sabbath—Fiction. 2. Jews—United States—Fiction. 3. Nursery schools—Fiction. 4. Schools—Fiction. 5. Imagination—Fiction.] I. Bosch, Nicole in den ill. II. Title.
PZ7.S6065 Sh 2001
[E]—dc21                                                                                        2001029625

Printed in China
4 – LP – 5/12/11

# The Shabbat Box

Lesley Simpson

illustrated by Nicole in den Bosch

KAR-BEN
PUBLISHING

Every Friday someone got to take home the Shabbat box. It was a shoebox covered in velvet with "Shabbat" written in Hebrew letters. Inside there were candlesticks, a kiddush cup, and a challah cover. Each week the teacher added fresh challah rolls with raisins.

Everyone loved the box.  There was only one problem.

There was only one box.

And there were 14 kids in the class.
There was Eli and Sarah and Noah and Rachel and

Sophie and Zachary and Sam and Rose and Ruth
and Ira and Naomi and Julia and Raffi and Miriam.

The rule was one turn per customer. And that meant Ira would have to wait until winter for his turn.

"How long until winter?" he asked his mother.
"After the leaves fall off the trees and snow comes," she answered.

"How long will that be?" asked Ira.

"About 14 weeks," said his mom.
"How long is 14 weeks?" he asked.
"About 98 sleeps," his mom explained.
"98 sleeps? That feels like forever!" said Ira.

After many, many sleeps, winter arrived, and it was finally Ira's turn. He put the Shabbat Box in his knapsack and started walking home.

But that Friday there was a bad snowstorm. The wind whipped his face. His eyes were so cold they felt like popsicles. His feet got soaked from snow falling into his boots.

When he finally made it home he was shivering. Inside the air was warm. His dad was making honey chicken. There was pea soup with noodles bubbling on the stove, and he could smell a chocolate cake baking in the oven.

Ira took off his knapsack. In the storm the flaps had opened and the Shabbat Box had fallen out. His lips trembled. He began to cry.

"What's wrong?"
asked his dad.

"The Shabbat Box is gone,"
he sobbed. "What can we do?"

They went outside to look for it. Their eyes stung, and they couldn't see through the blowing snow. Cars were sliding, and people were slipping on the ice. "We'd better go back inside," his dad said.

Ira began sobbing again. "There is only one Shabbat Box, and I have lost it and I am going to be in trouble."

He didn't want to eat the soup or the chicken, or even the chocolate cake.

"How do you think we can solve this?" his mother asked.

Ira thought. He thought so much his head hurt. He felt miserable.

Saturday afternoon he was lying on his bed.
He saw the empty box from his snow-boots.
"I know what I'm going to do," he whispered
to his stuffed animals. "I will make a new
Shabbat box! It will be a surprise."

After Havdalah, he put a "Do Not Enter"
sign on his bedroom door. He took his art
kit and big camping flashlight down from
his closet. He pulled out the box.

He decorated it with
purple velvet and
shiny sparkles.

He turned his plasticine snakes
into candlesticks.

He made a memory game with pictures of challahs, candlesticks, wine cups, and people singing.  He painted grapes on his water cup and turned it into a kiddush cup.

He painted his pillow case and turned it into a giant challah cover.

He stayed up all night painting, pasting, and designing everything. He worked by flashlight under the covers of his bed. By the time he went to sleep it was almost morning.

On Sunday he put lollipops and taffy and hard candies and chocolates into the box because Shabbat should be sweet.

He wrapped the box in plastic in case it fell into a snowbank again.

Monday was his turn for show-and-tell. As he unwrapped the box, kids gathered around him.

He told them the story of how he lost the box in the snow and how he tried to find it. He told them how upset he was, but he left out the part about crying because he didn't want them to think he was a baby.

Then he told them how he made a new Shabbat box for the class.

He took a deep breath.

"I hope you like it," Ira said.

He opened the lid.

Everyone peered inside. All the kids were jumping up and down saying they wanted to take Ira's box home and eat the sweets and play the memory game and try out the cool candlesticks.

"I have something for show-and-tell, too," said the teacher.
"But show-and-tell is for kids," Rachel protested.

"Last Friday, the day of the storm, I forgot my mittens," the teacher explained.

"So I went back to school to look for them because my hands were freezing.  I saw something peeking out of the snow."

She took a slightly crumpled box out of the cupboard.

It was the Shabbat Box.

"The bad news is that the challah rolls were soggy," the teacher said.

"But the good news is that the box dried."

"Now we have two Shabbat boxes!" said Ira.

"Only 49 more sleeps until my next turn."

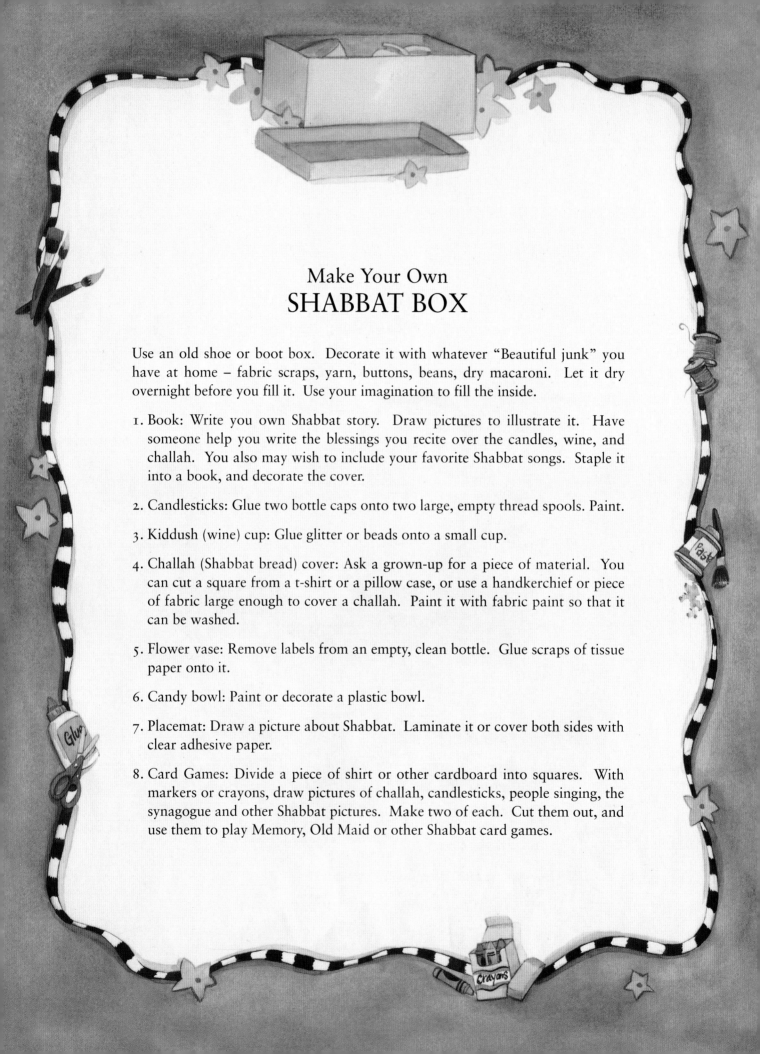

# Make Your Own
# SHABBAT BOX

Use an old shoe or boot box. Decorate it with whatever "Beautiful junk" you have at home – fabric scraps, yarn, buttons, beans, dry macaroni. Let it dry overnight before you fill it. Use your imagination to fill the inside.

1. Book: Write you own Shabbat story. Draw pictures to illustrate it. Have someone help you write the blessings you recite over the candles, wine, and challah. You also may wish to include your favorite Shabbat songs. Staple it into a book, and decorate the cover.

2. Candlesticks: Glue two bottle caps onto two large, empty thread spools. Paint.

3. Kiddush (wine) cup: Glue glitter or beads onto a small cup.

4. Challah (Shabbat bread) cover: Ask a grown-up for a piece of material. You can cut a square from a t-shirt or a pillow case, or use a handkerchief or piece of fabric large enough to cover a challah. Paint it with fabric paint so that it can be washed.

5. Flower vase: Remove labels from an empty, clean bottle. Glue scraps of tissue paper onto it.

6. Candy bowl: Paint or decorate a plastic bowl.

7. Placemat: Draw a picture about Shabbat. Laminate it or cover both sides with clear adhesive paper.

8. Card Games: Divide a piece of shirt or other cardboard into squares. With markers or crayons, draw pictures of challah, candlesticks, people singing, the synagogue and other Shabbat pictures. Make two of each. Cut them out, and use them to play Memory, Old Maid or other Shabbat card games.